The Enormous Turnip

Jackie Walter and Mark Chambers

W

Once upon a time, an old farmer and his wife grew a fine field full of turnips on their farm.

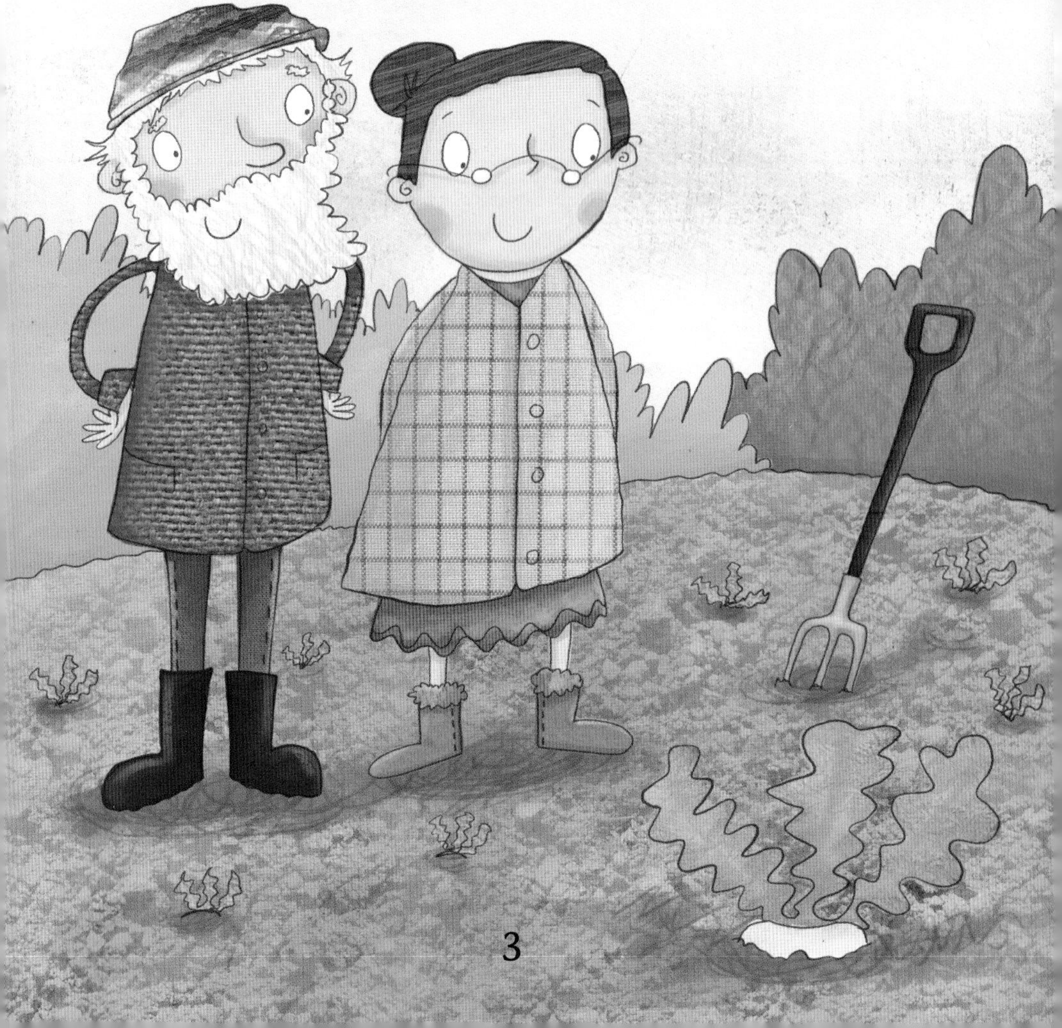

All of the turnips were big and juicy, but one turnip looked enormous.

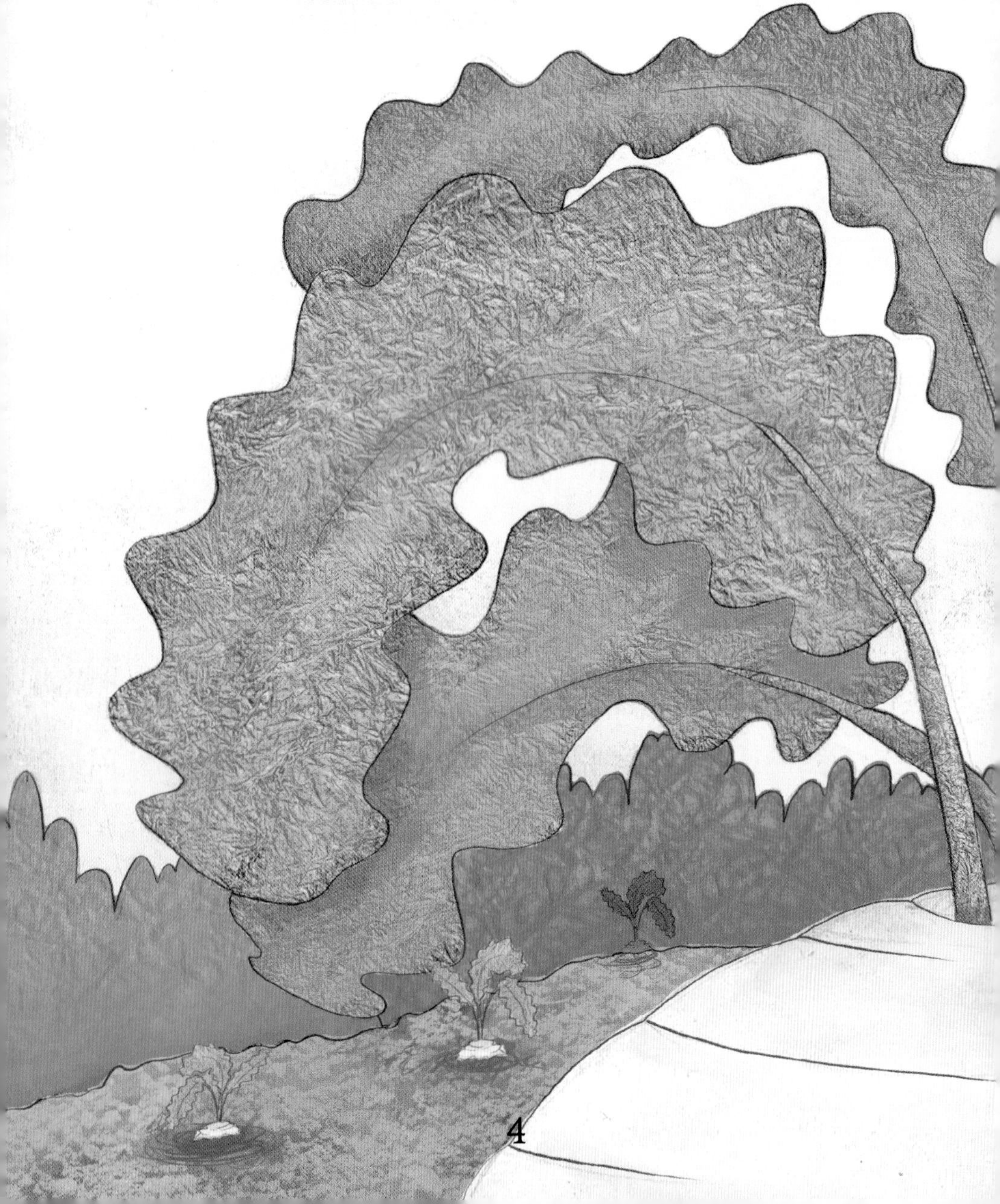

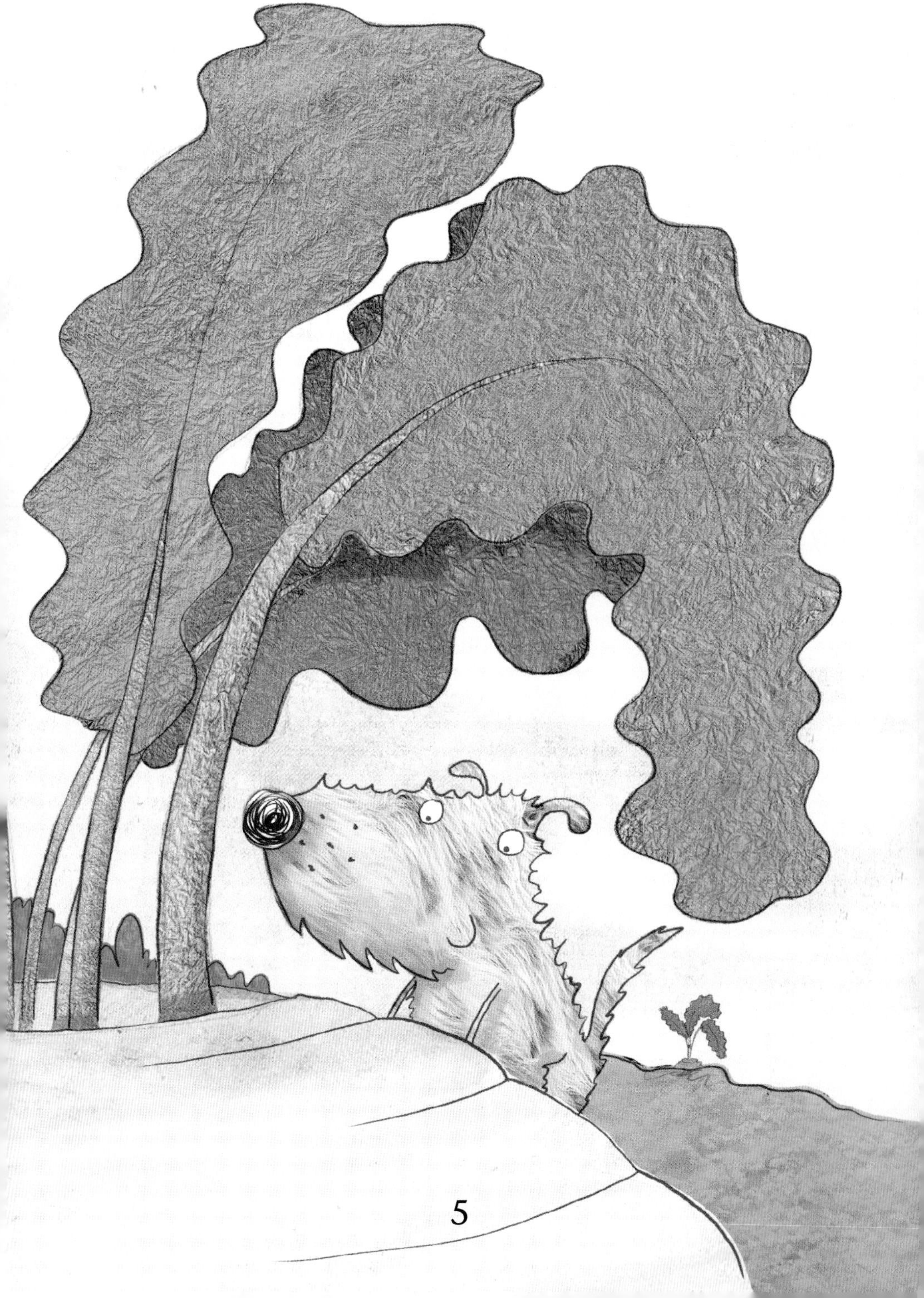

"It's time to pull up that enormous turnip," said the farmer. "It looks almost as big as a bear!"

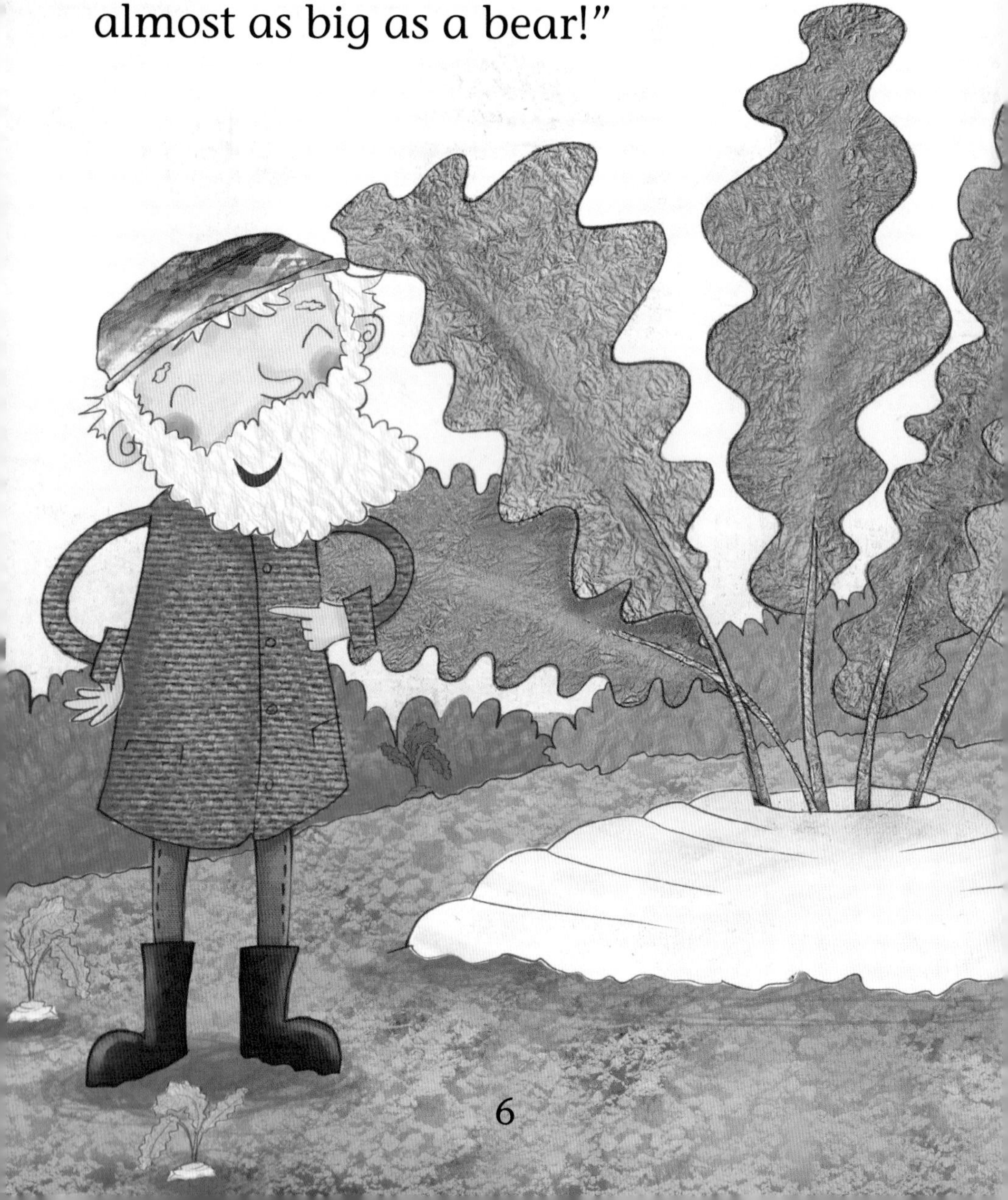

"Yes," agreed his wife. "Then we can have turnip soup for supper, as long as I can find a pot big enough to cook it in!"

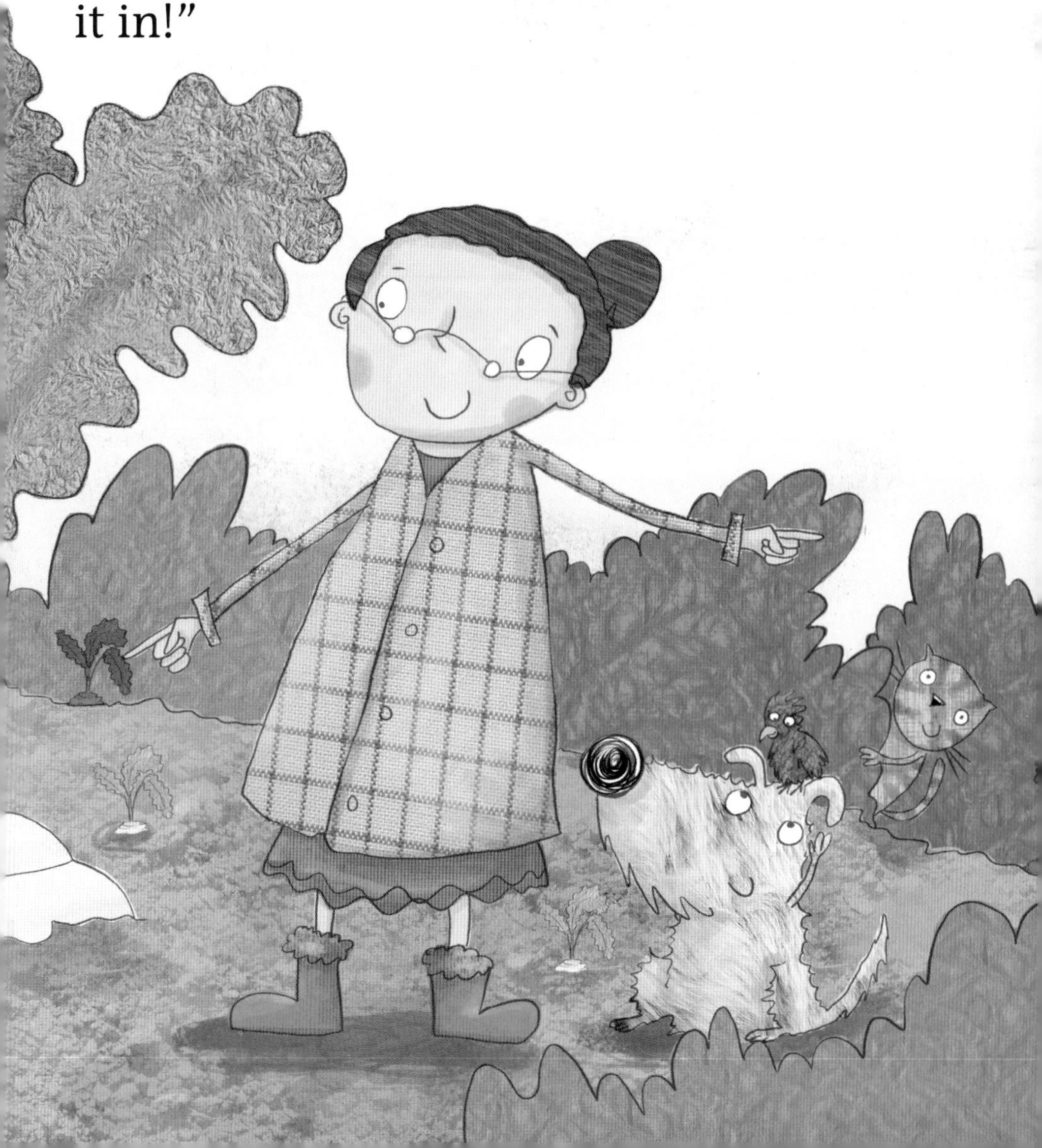

The farmer gave the enormous turnip a gentle tug. The turnip did not move even one little bit.

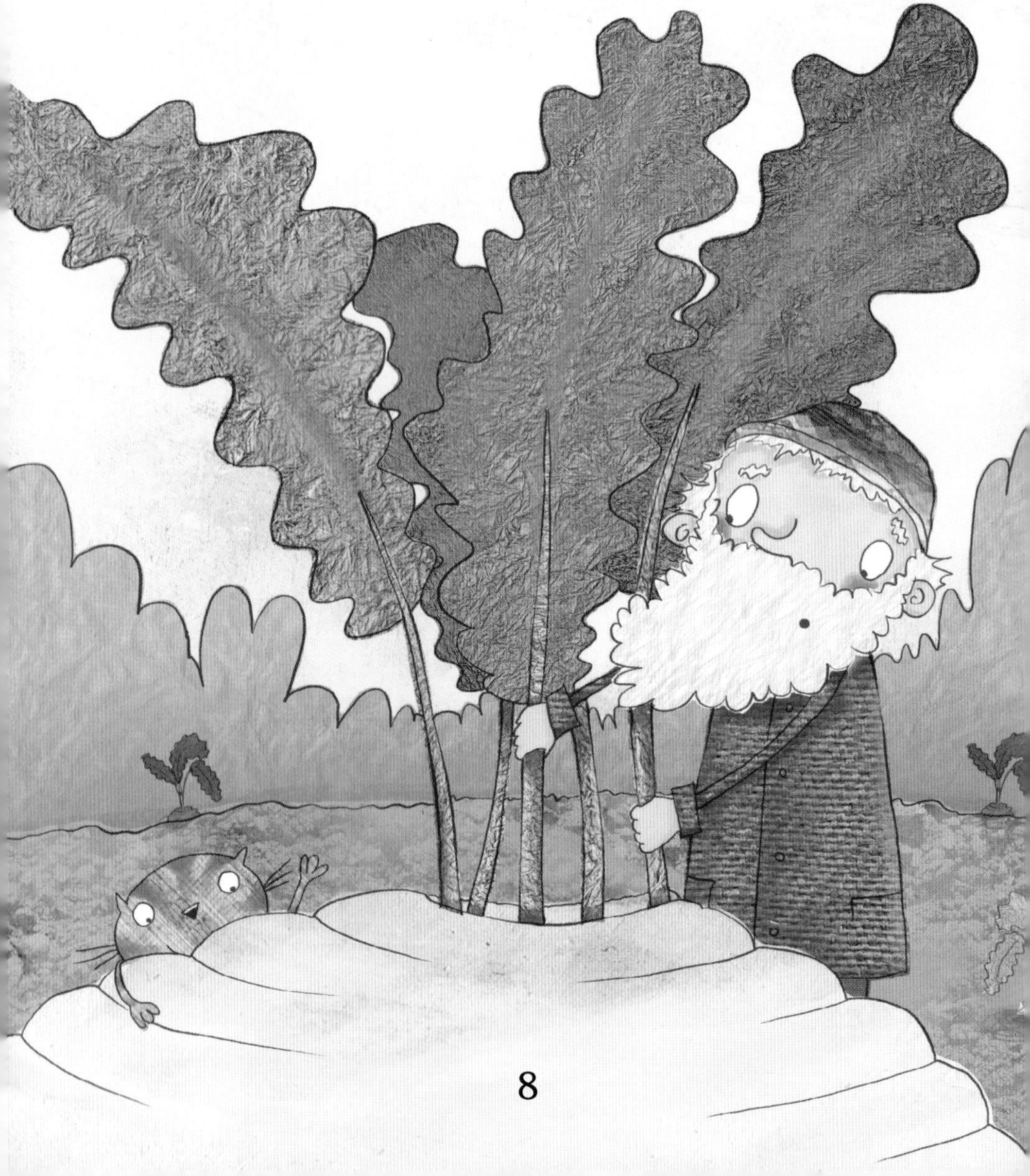

The farmer scratched his head.

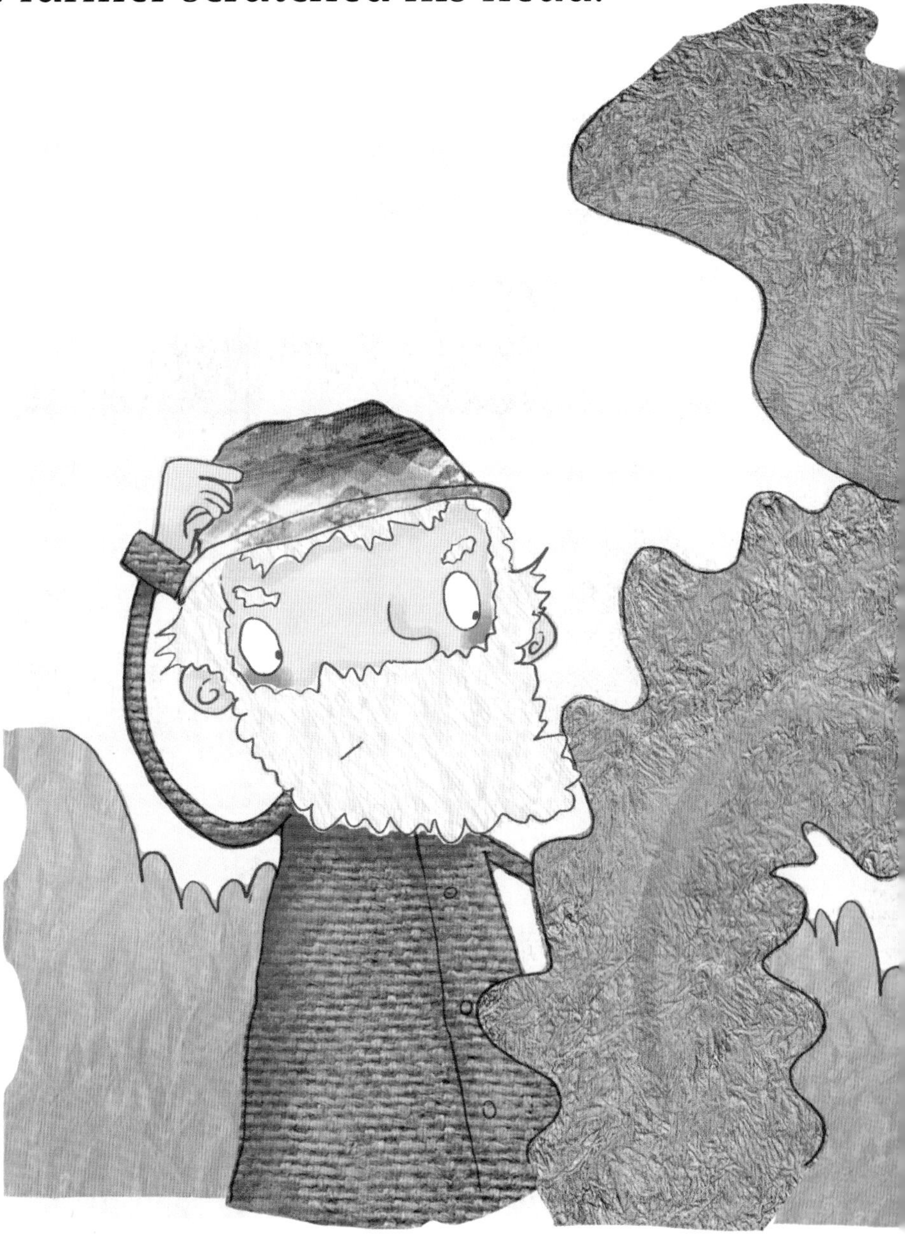

The farmer tried again. He pulled and pulled. Still the turnip did not move. So he leaned back and pulled with all his might.

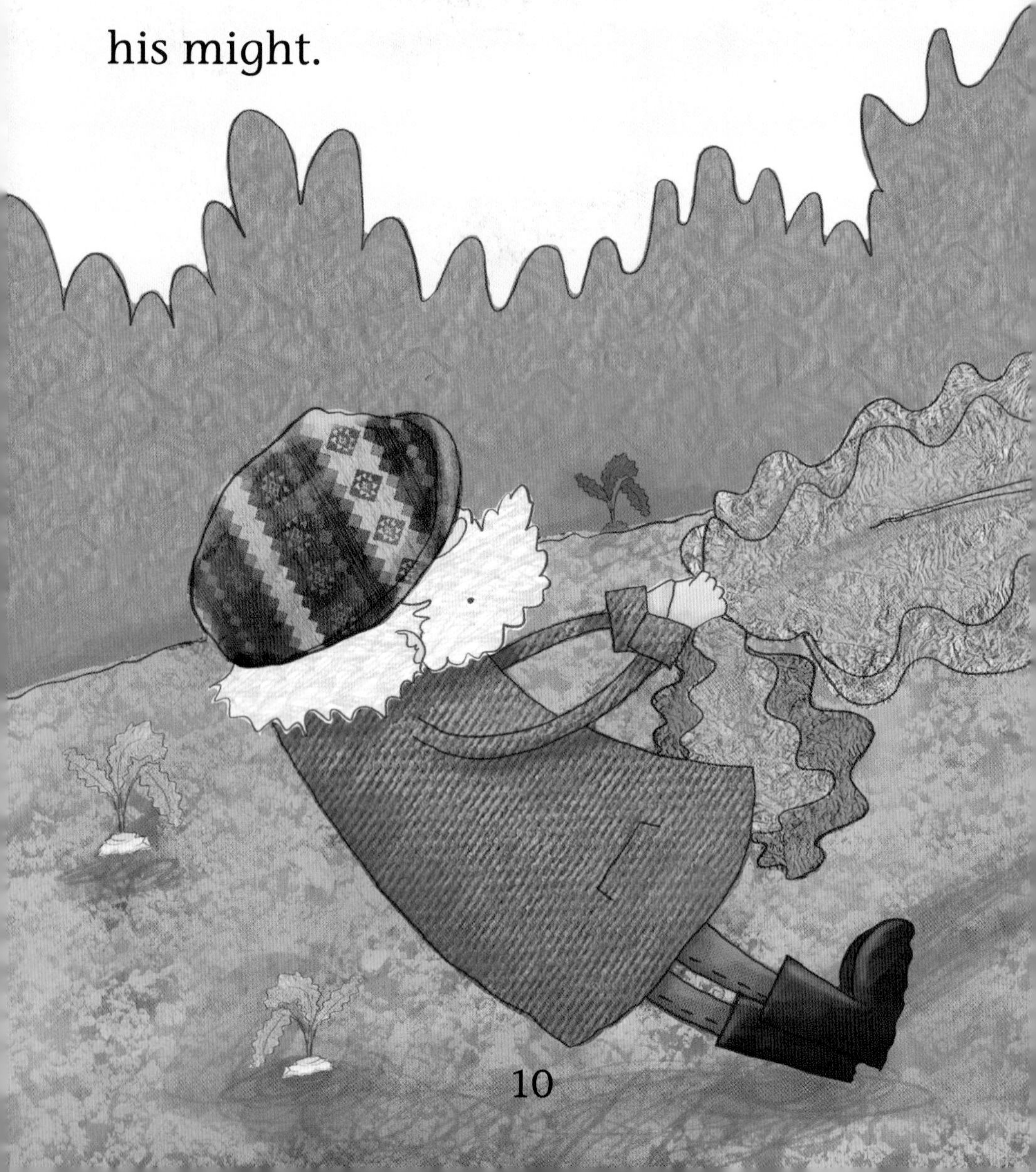

But the turnip was stuck.

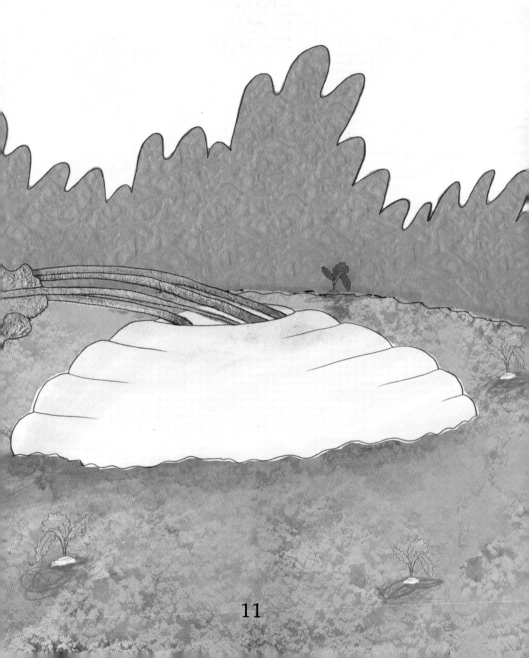

The farmer called to his wife for help. She grabbed her husband and together they pulled and pulled with all their might.

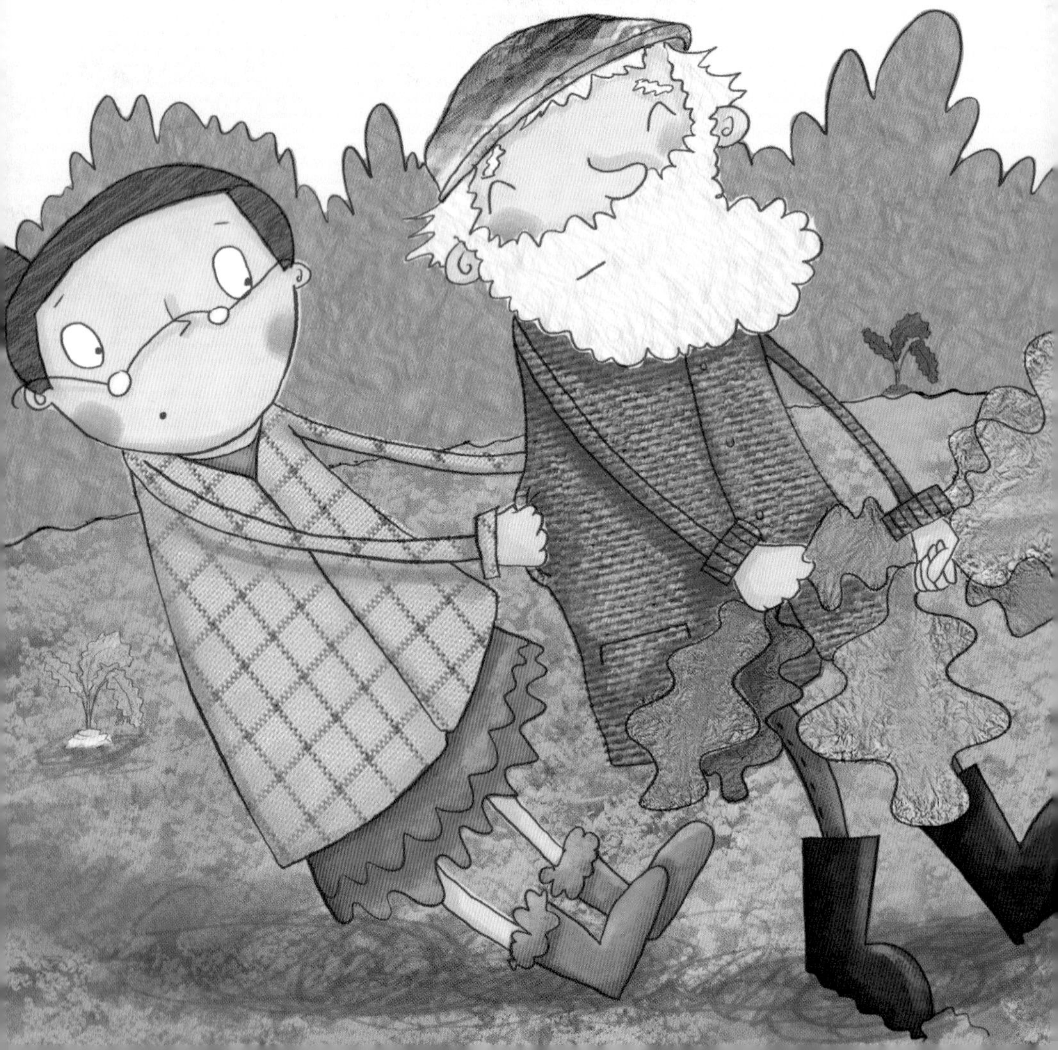

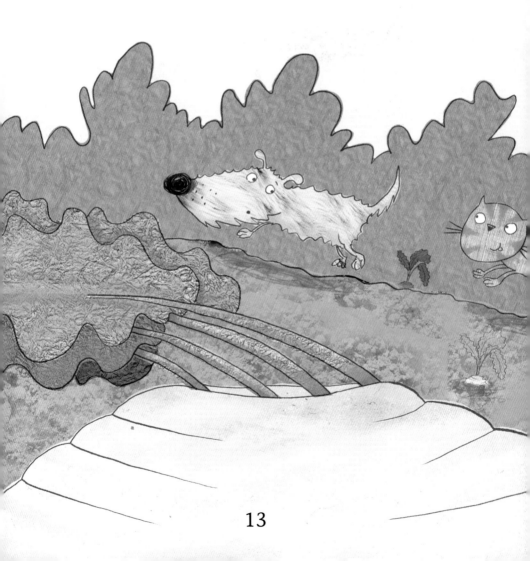

The farmer and his wife fell back in the mud. Still the turnip did not move.

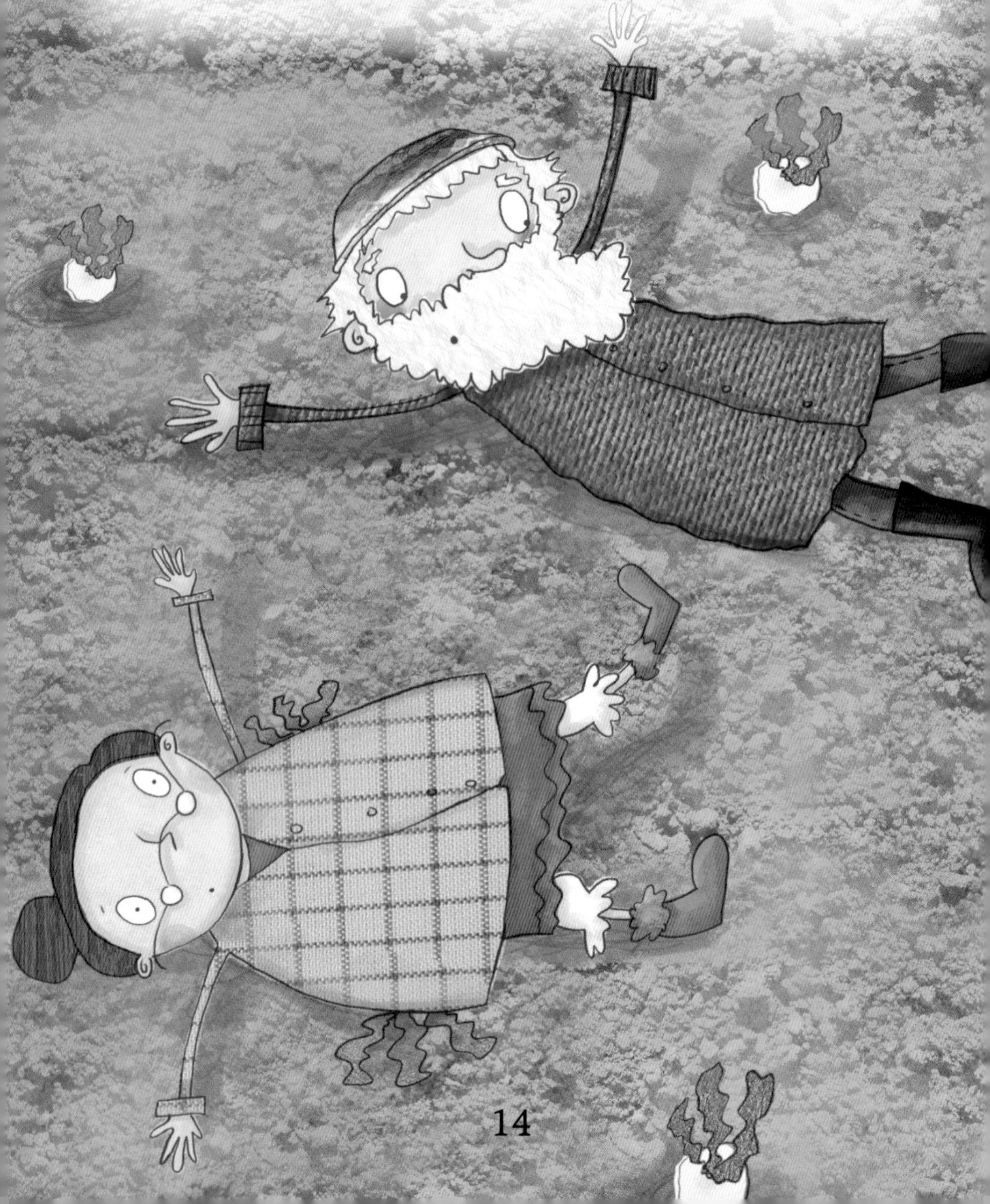

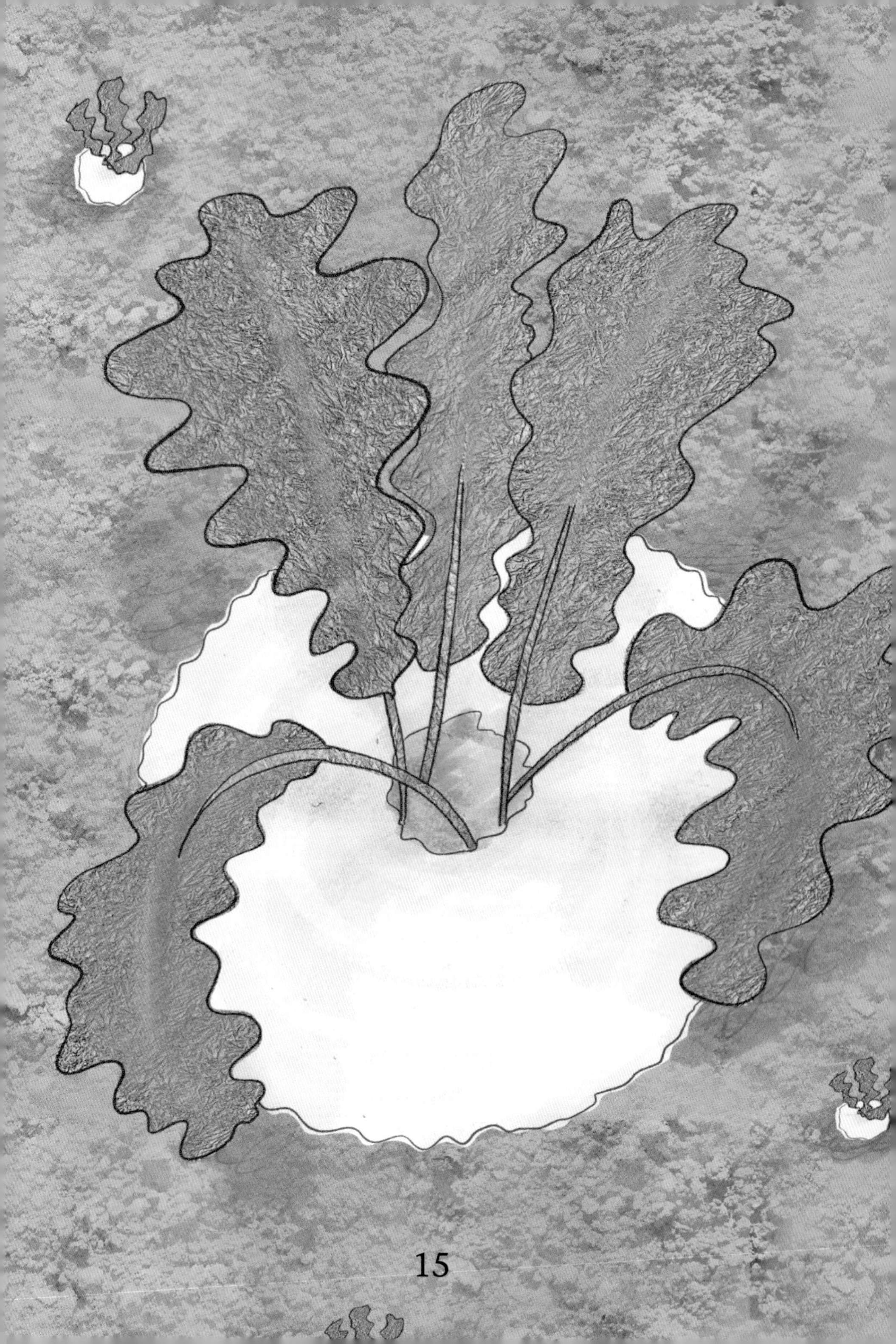

The farmer's wife whistled to the dog for help. The dog grabbed the farmer's wife.

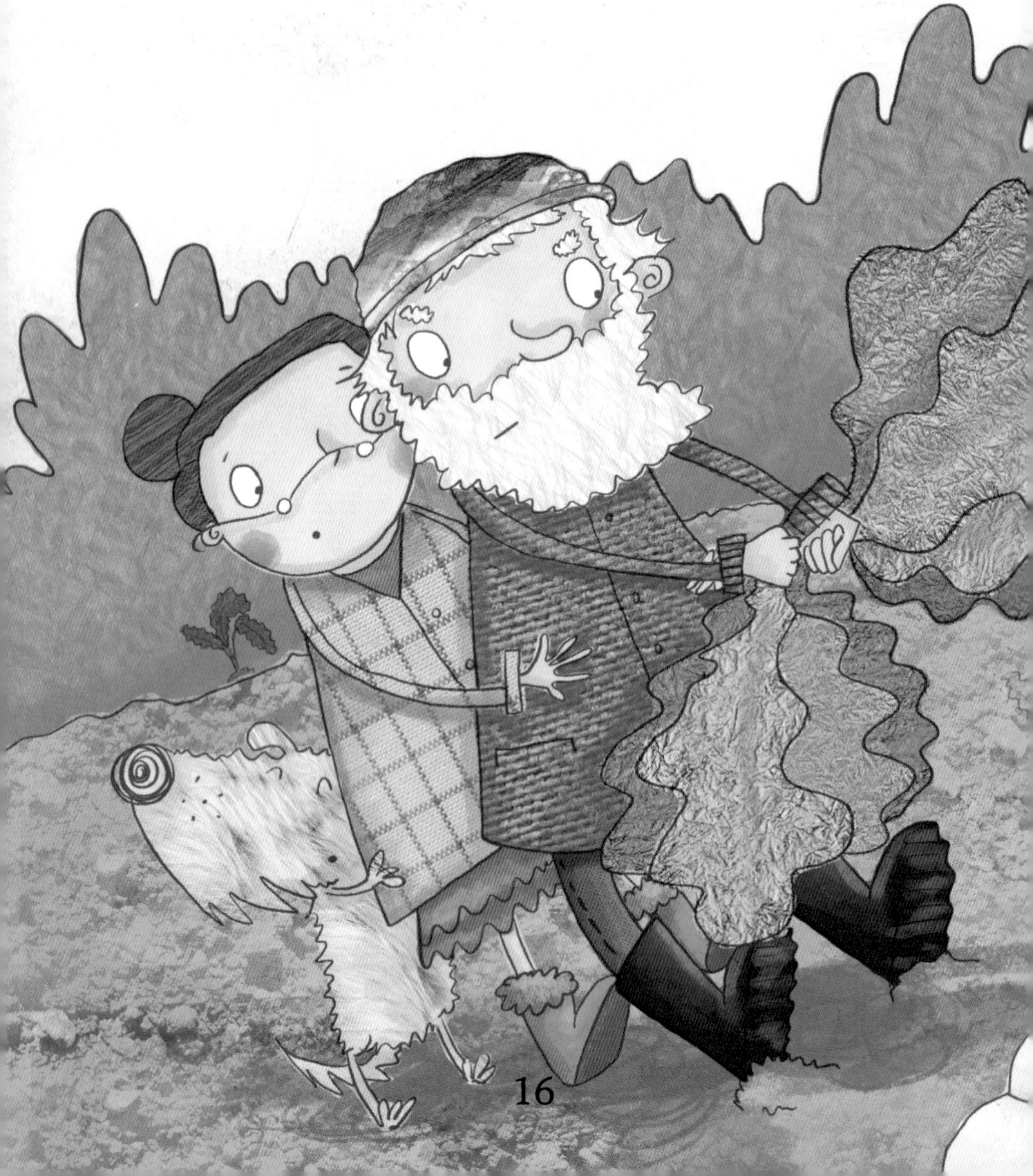

Together, the farmer, his wife and the dog pulled and pulled with all their might.

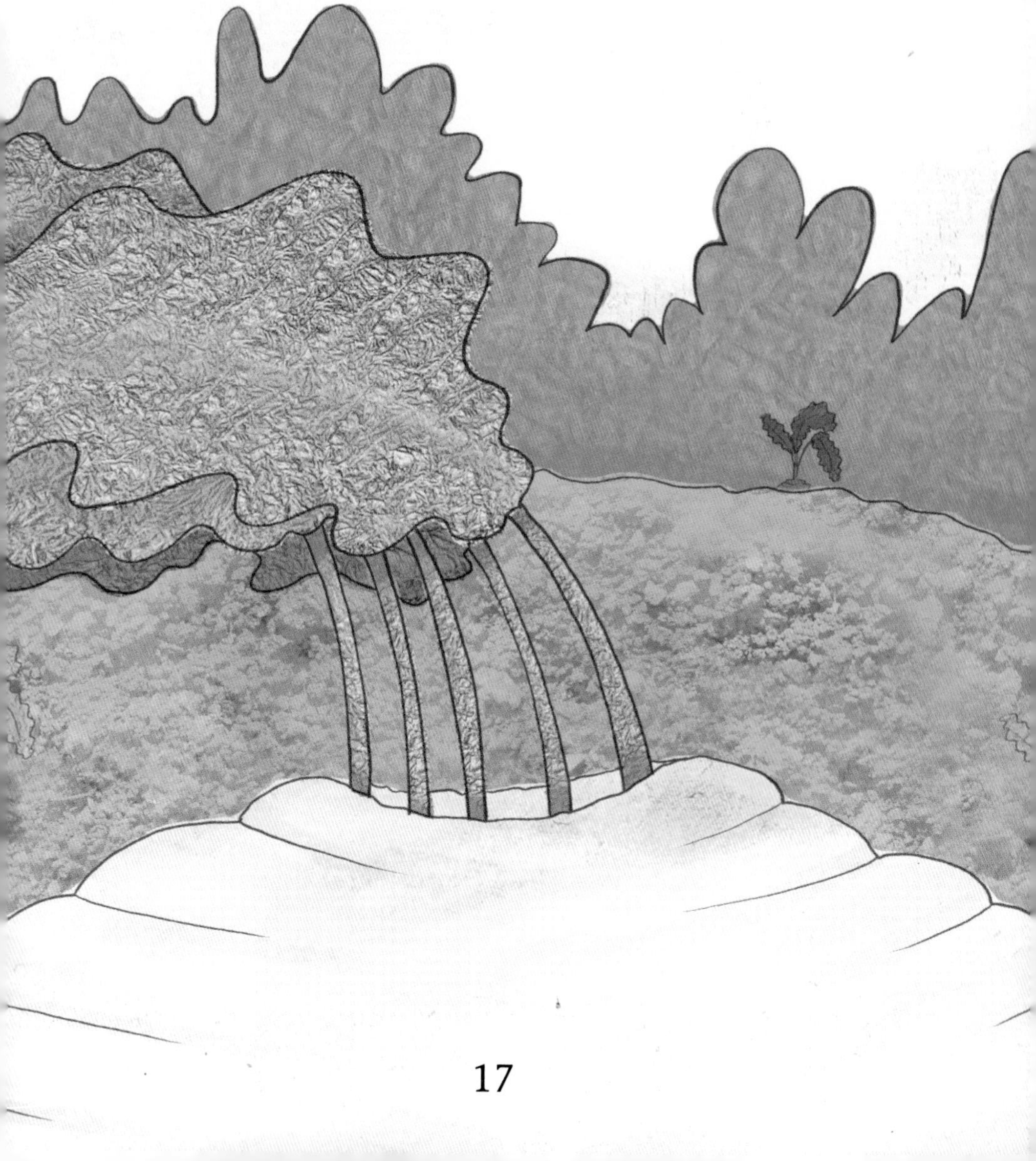

The farmer, his wife and the dog fell back in the mud. Still the turnip did not move.

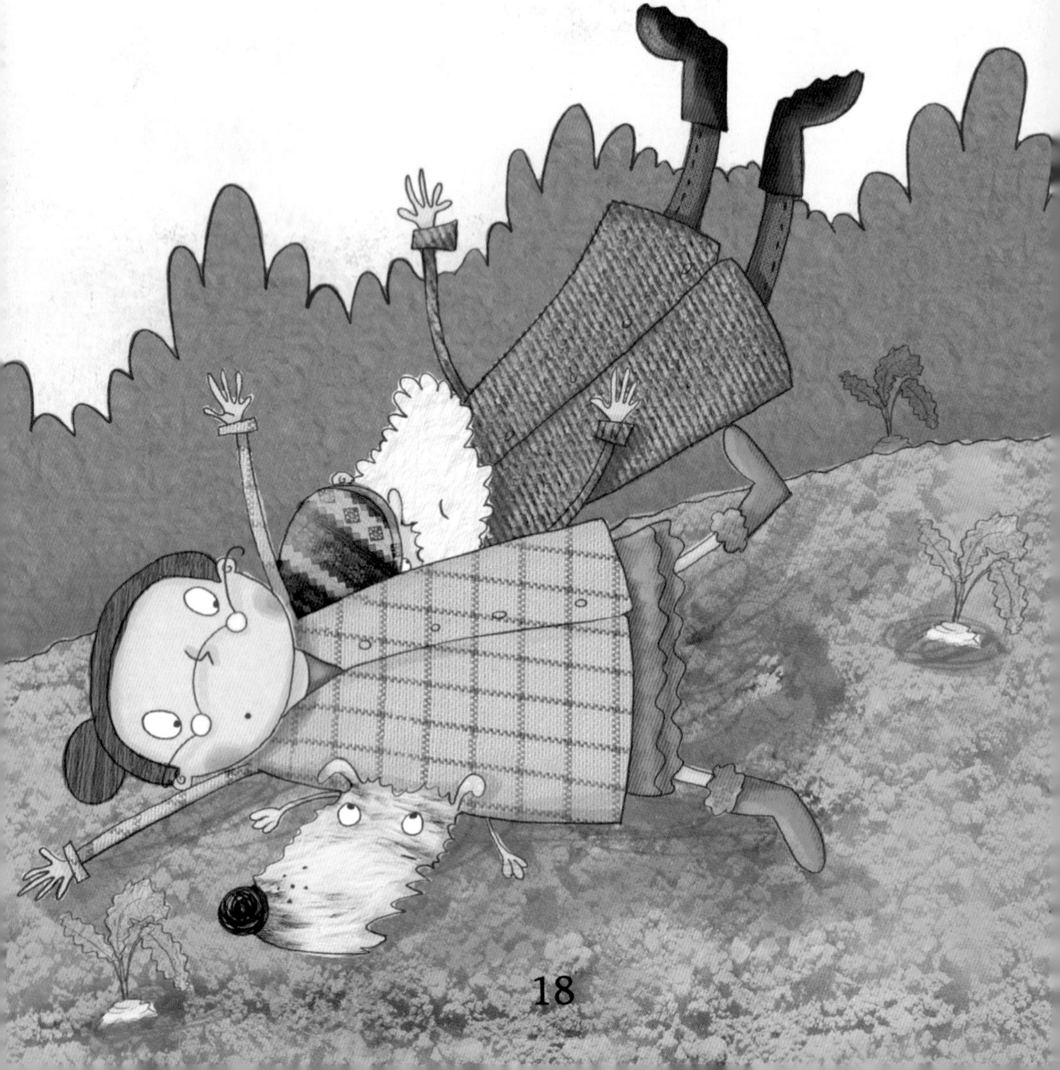

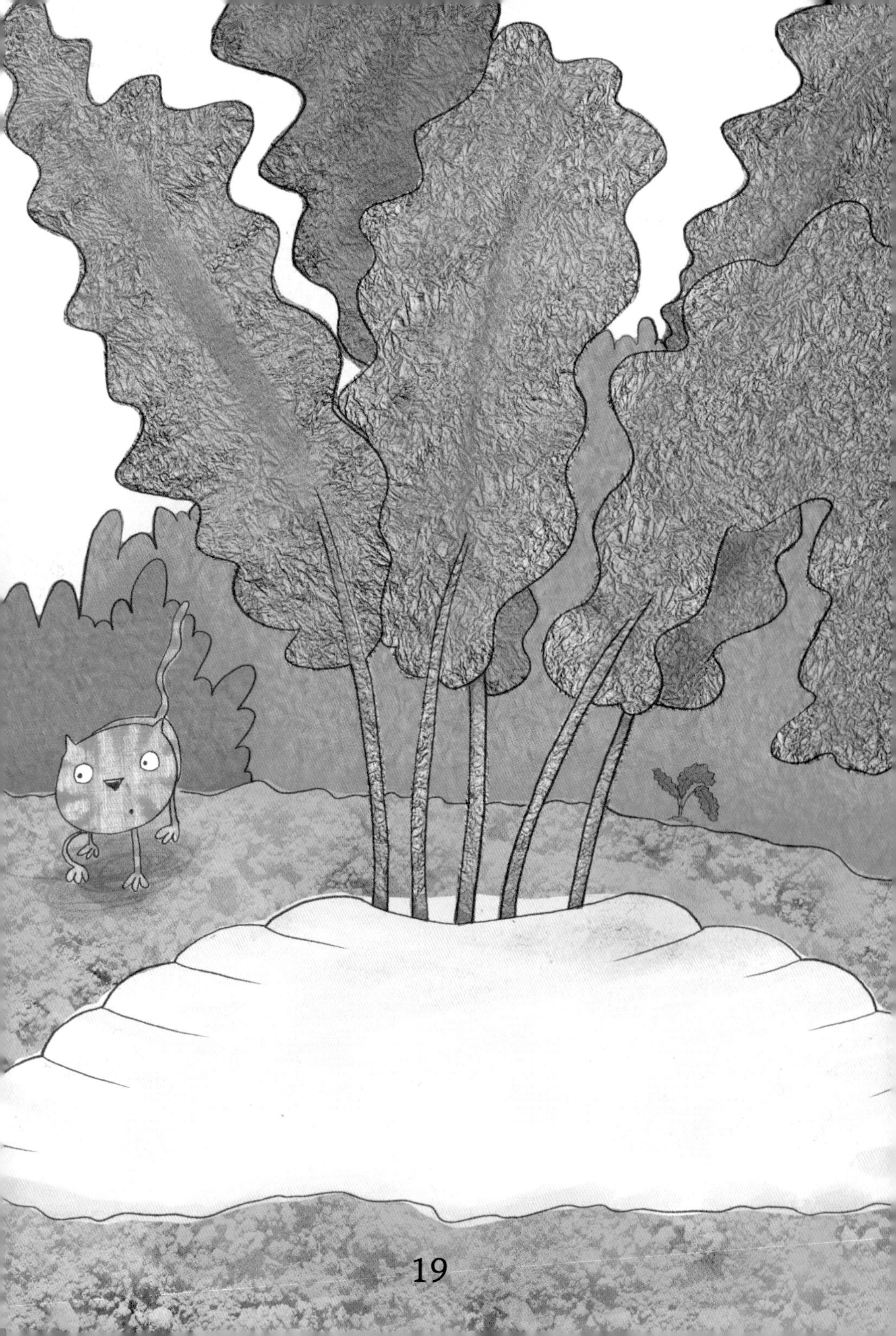

So the dog barked to the cat for help.

The cat grabbed the dog's tail.

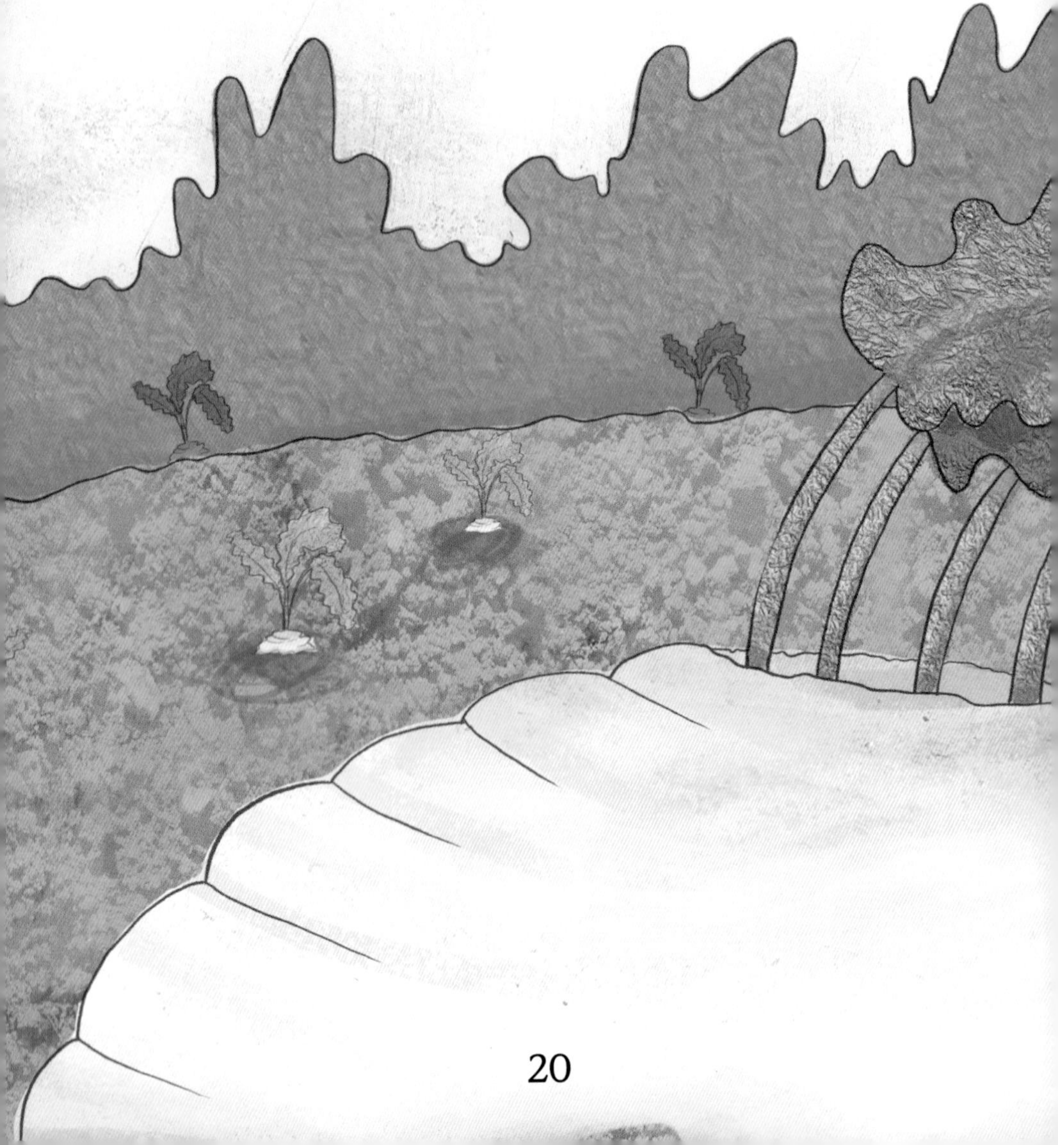

Together, the farmer, his wife, the dog and the cat pulled and pulled with all their might.

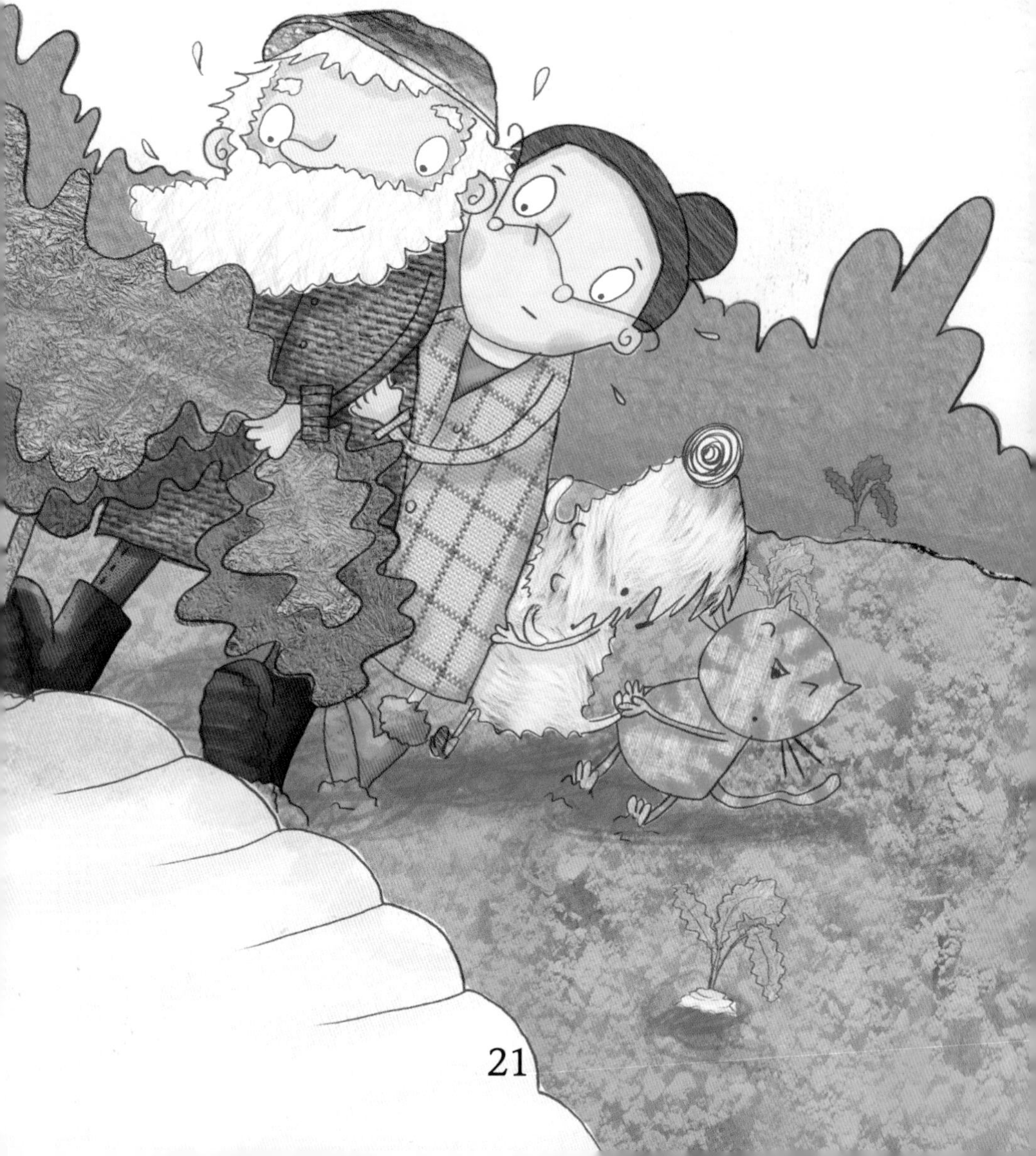

The farmer, his wife, the dog and the cat fell back in the mud. Still the turnip did not move.

"It's no good. This turnip is stuck. I don't think we'll ever pull it up!" sighed the farmer miserably.

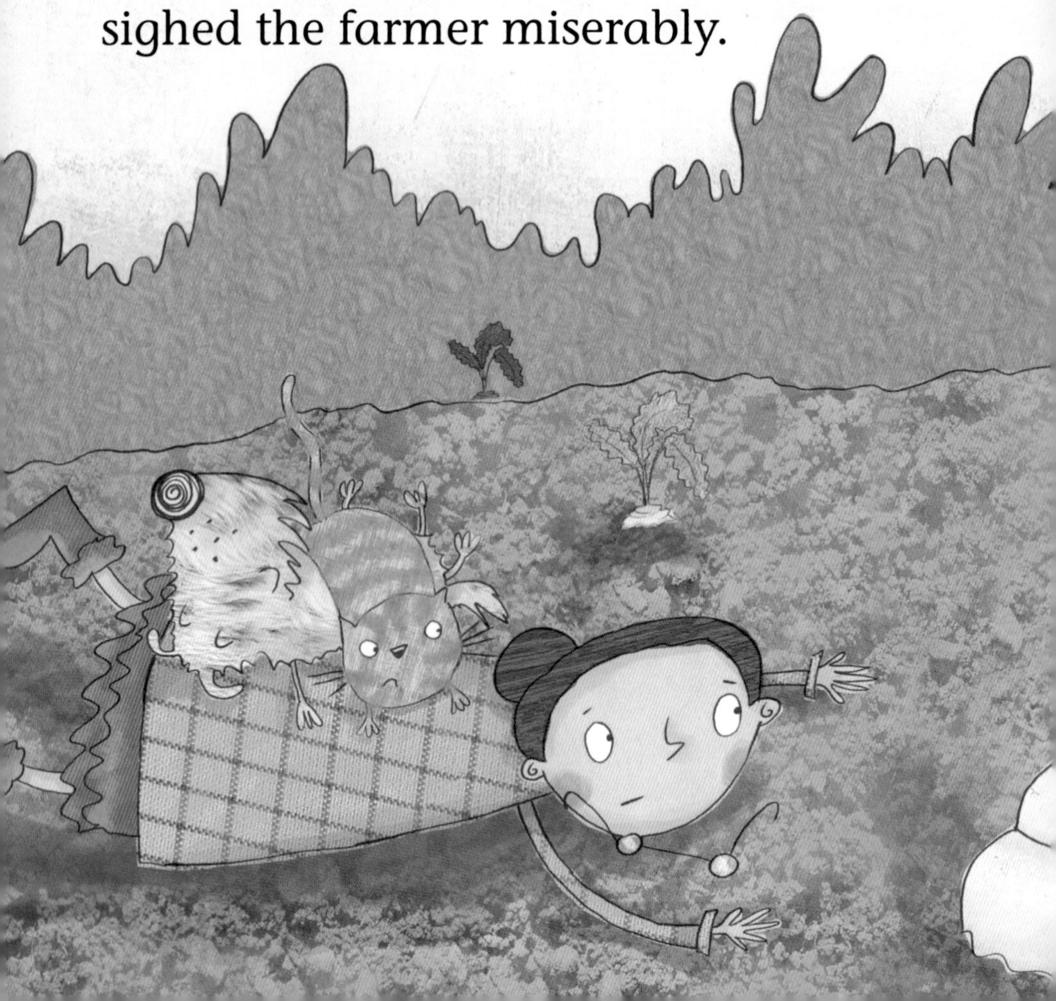

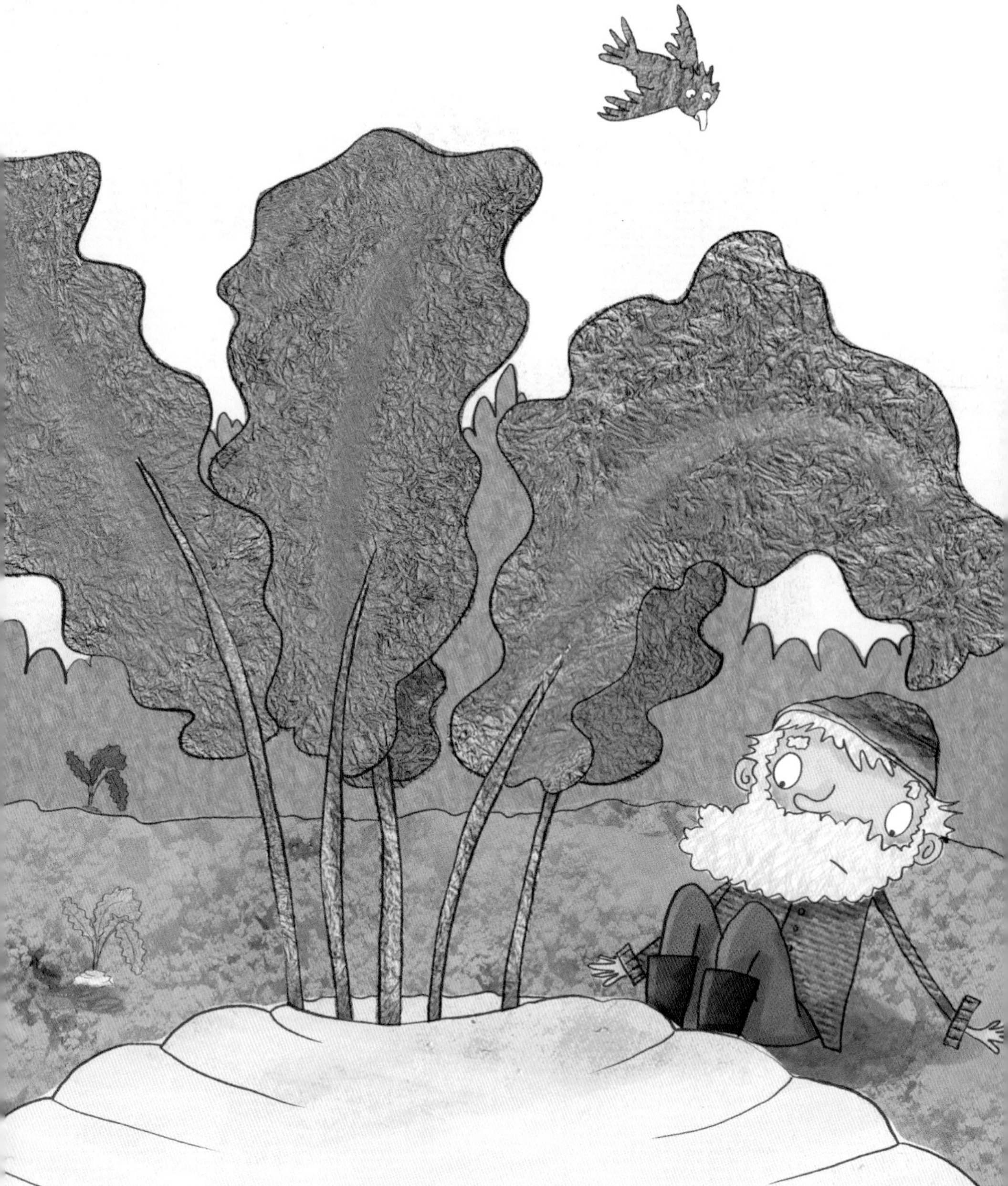

Then the cat had a good idea. She meowed to a little bird for help. The little bird grabbed the cat's ear.

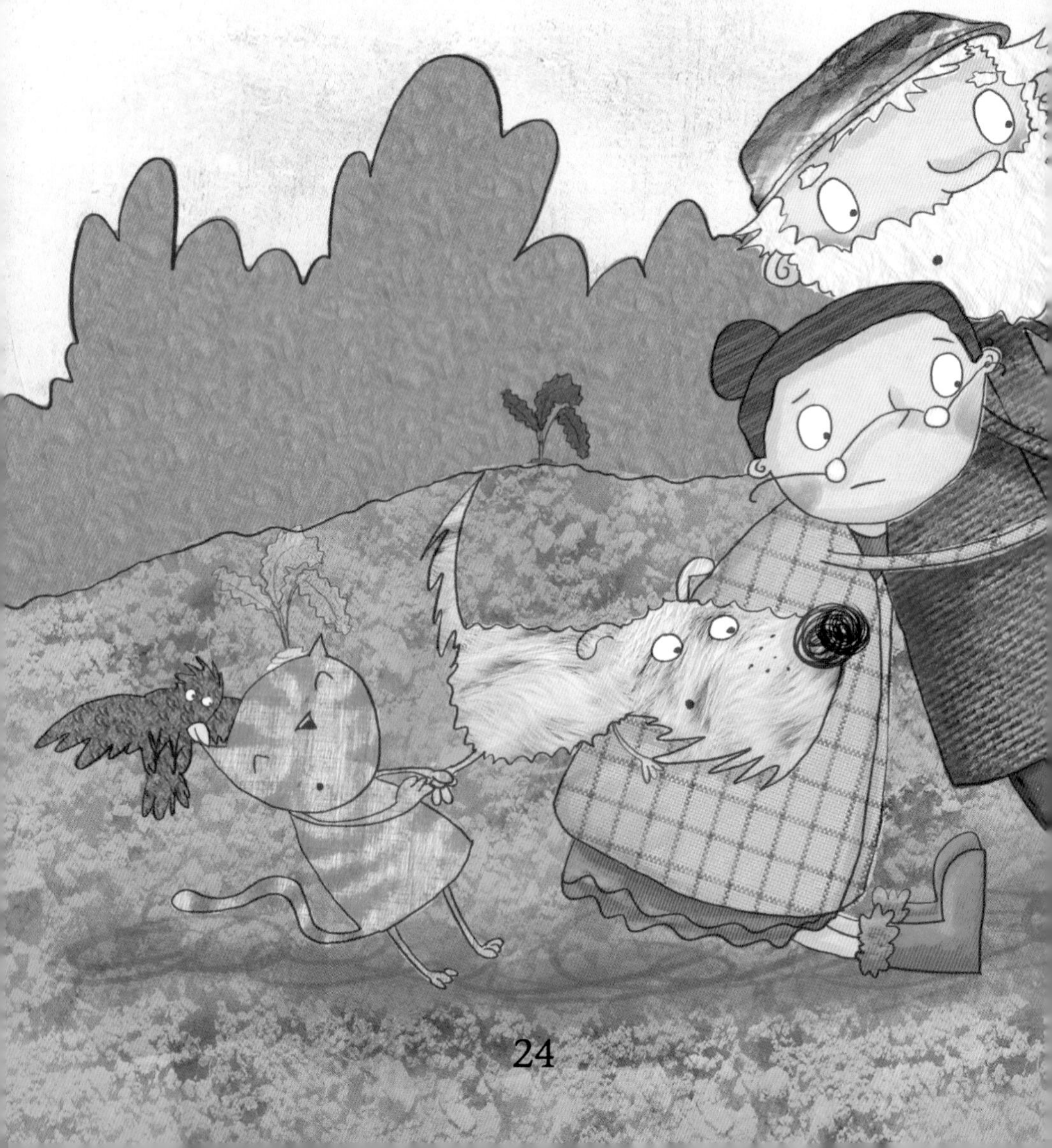

Together, the farmer, his wife, the dog, the cat and the little bird pulled and pulled and pulled...

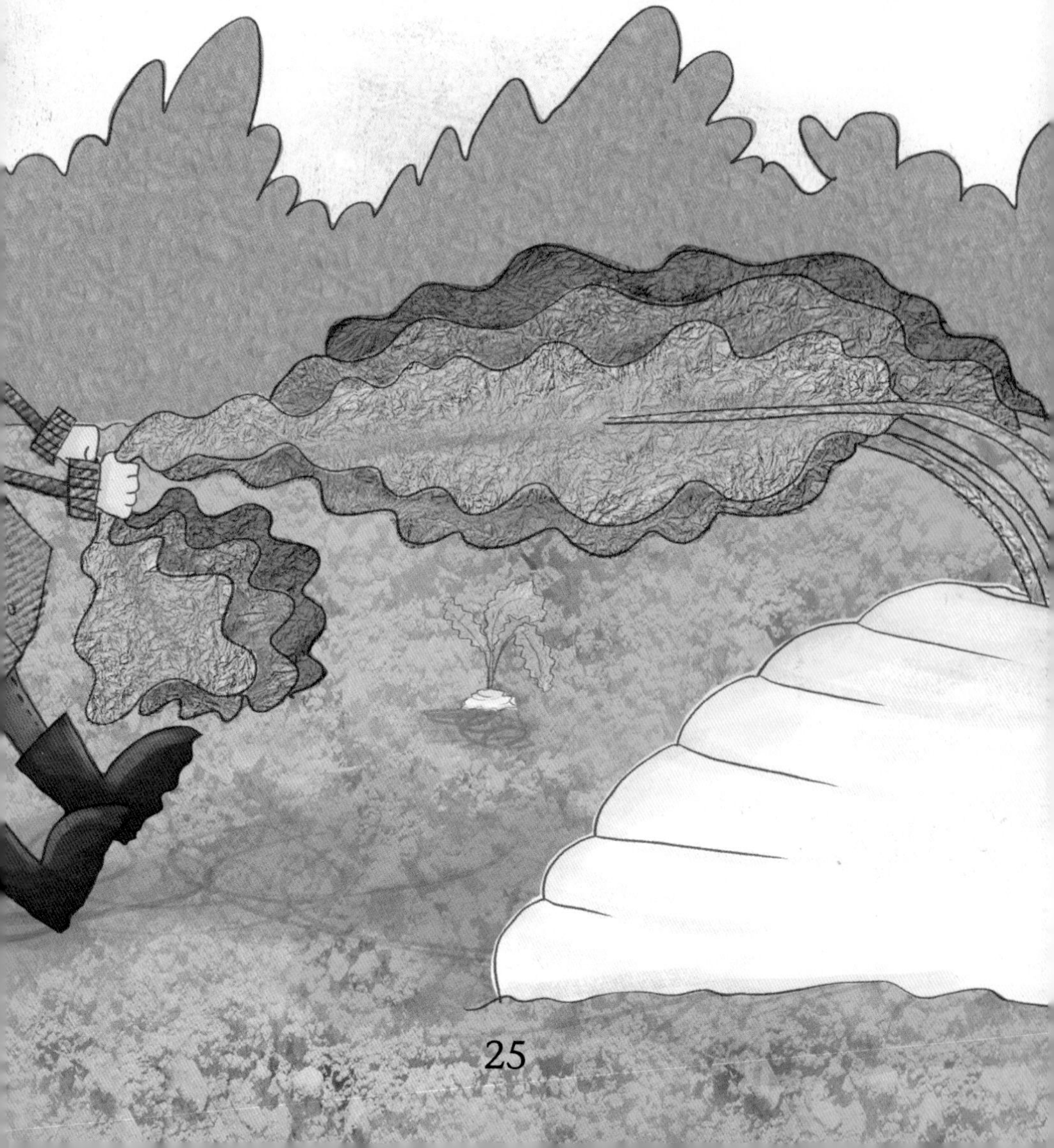

Up came the enormous turnip
with an enormous POP!
It was even bigger
than a bear!

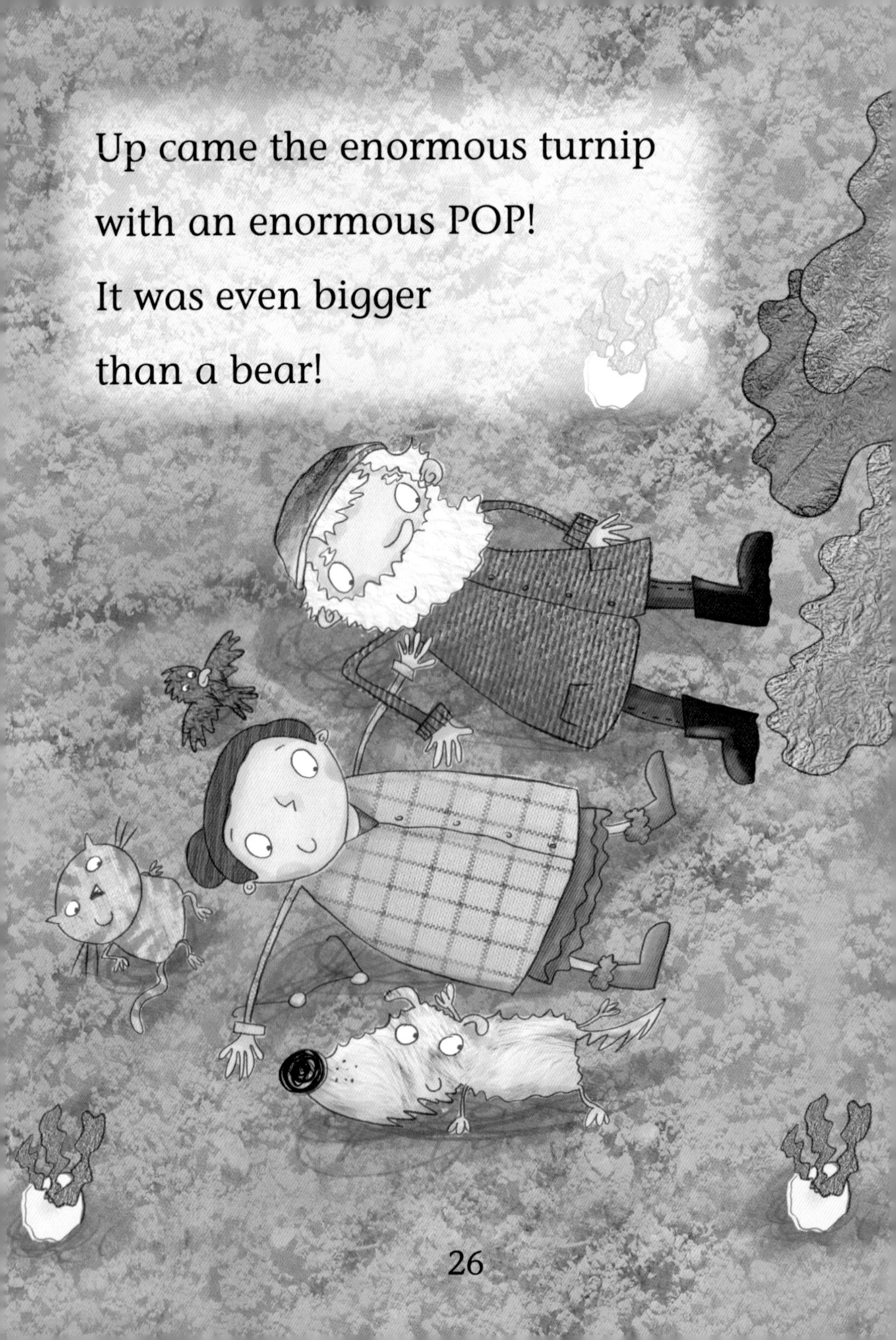

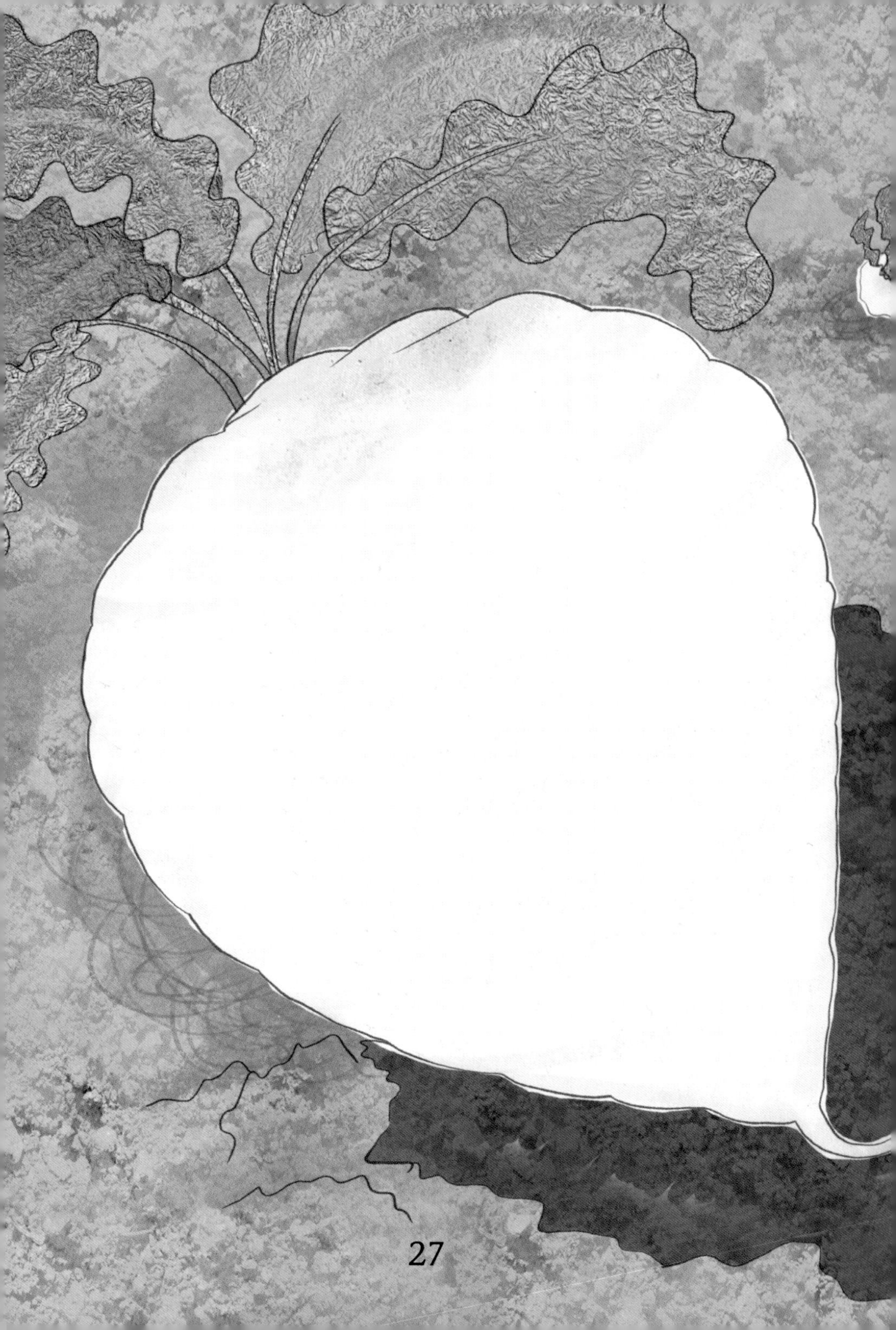

That evening, the farmer's wife found an enormous pot for the enormous turnip, and they all had turnip soup for supper.

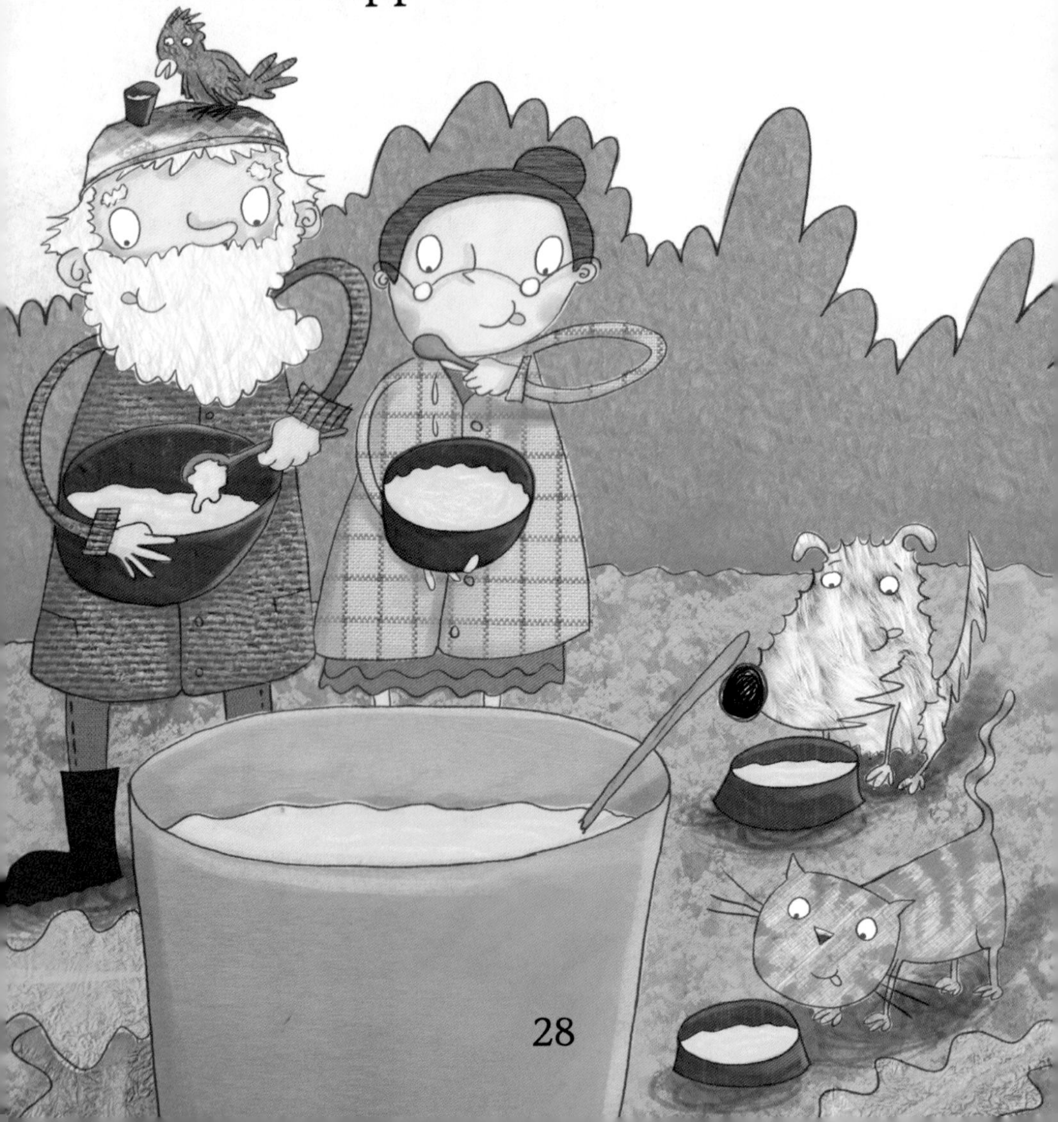

The next day, they had turnip soup for breakfast.

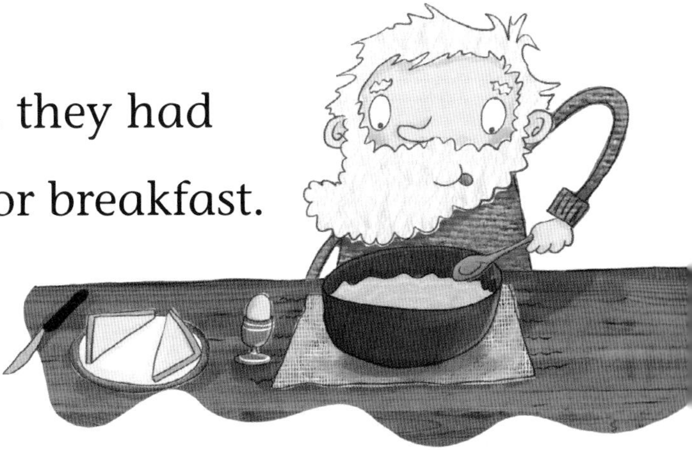

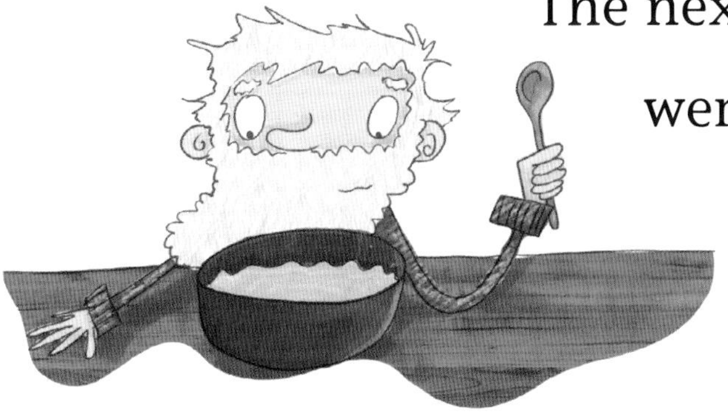

The next week, they were still eating turnip soup for lunch.

And people say that they still have turnip soup to this very day!

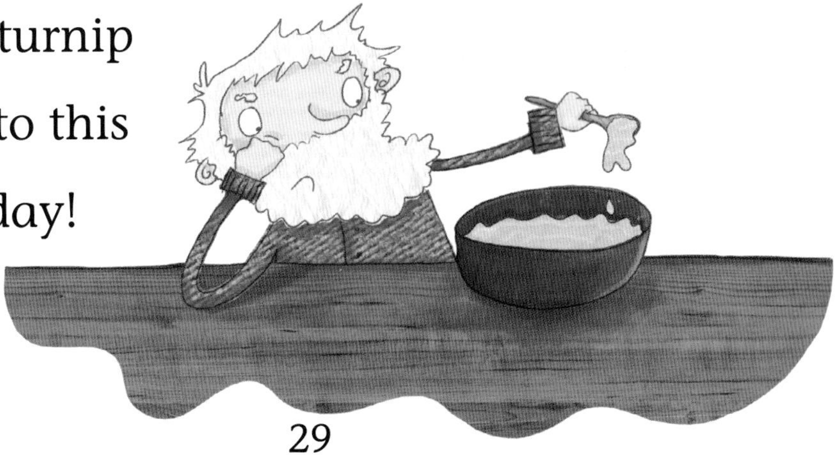

About the story

The Enormous Turnip is a folk tale from Russia. It was first published in 1863. Sometimes different people or animals feature in the story.

One thing remains the same, however, in all the versions. It is always the weakest and smallest creature who makes the difference and allows the enormous turnip to be pulled from the ground.

Be in the story!

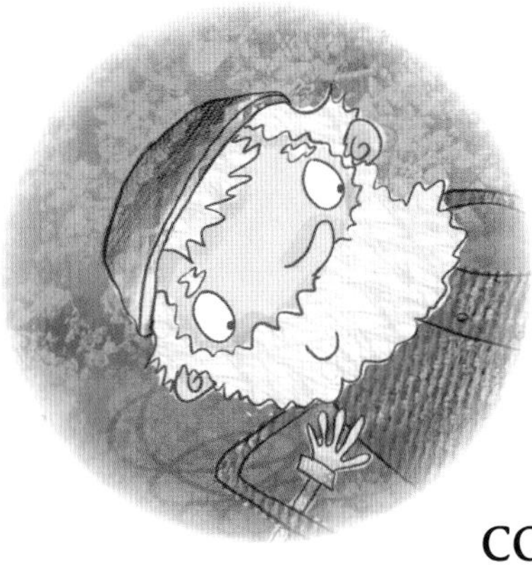

Imagine you are the farmer. How do you feel when the enormous turnip comes out of the ground?

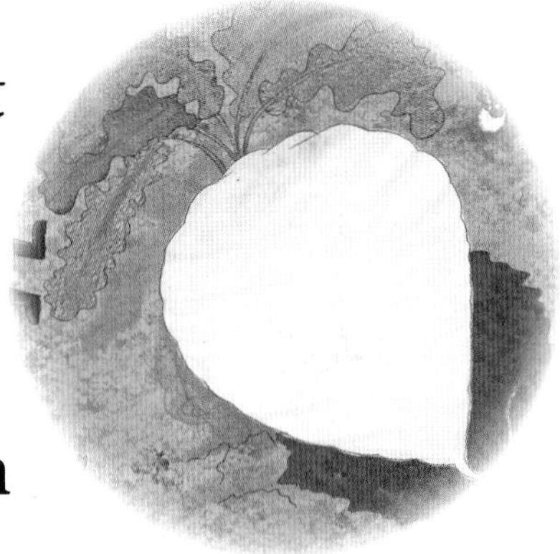

Now imagine that it isn't a turnip that is pulled up. What else could it be? Can you give the story a different ending?

Franklin Watts
First published in Great Britain in 2015 by The Watts Publishing Group

Copyright © The Watts Publishing Group 2015

Series Editor: Jackie Hamley
Series Advisor: Catherine Glavina
Series Designer: Cathryn Gilbert

A CIP catalogue record for this book is available
from the British Library.

The artwork for this story first appeared in
Leapfrog: The Enormous Turnip

ISBN 978 1 4451 4440 5 (hbk)
ISBN 978 1 4451 4442 9 (pbk)
ISBN 978 1 4451 4441 2 (library ebook)
ISBN 978 1 4451 4443 6 (ebook)

Printed in China

Franklin Watts
An imprint of
Hachette Children's Group
Part of The Watts Publishing Group
Carmelite House
50 Victoria Embankment
London EC4Y 0DZ

An Hachette UK Company
www.hachette.co.uk

www.franklinwatts.co.uk

FSC
www.fsc.org
MIX
Paper from
responsible sources
FSC® C104740